Work? Shmurk!

By Melanie Atkinson

Table of Contents

Team Building

"Just think of it as a team-building exercise. We'll all be there," your coworker tells you.

Hopefully, it'll be better than 'trust falls' or the inexorable panic of trying to find one interesting, safe for work fact to tell a circle of new colleagues.

"Meet us here on Friday night."

An address sent in a text message. A sly grin from the girl who sits at the desk next to you. Whispers and pointed looks through the kettle's steam as you walk past the break room. You think no more about it as your brain fills up with the minutiae of the new tasks of your new role in your new job as you try to be the new you.

Friday night is cold. After returning to your flat, you want to vegetate in your pyjamas, turn into a feral goblin with hands sticky from snack dust and face cold and clean beneath a eucalyptus mask until you fall asleep to the soothing lullaby of the adverts. Sighing, you decide to make the effort. You wrinkle your nose at the thought of having to play nice and dash your foundation around the scowl.

Wobbling over the cobblestones, desperate not to turn an ankle atop your favourite high heels, you hope it's a pub or a trendy wine bar where alcohol will soothe the anxiety of getting-to-know-you bullshit small talk. It's not.

Outside a municipal-looking building at the address you have been given is a gaggle of giggling women.

They remind you of a cluster of clucking chickens, fluffy and seraphic on the outside, but willing to peck each other's eyes with razor sharp beaks at any perceived slight.

"Laydeez Night!" crows the sandwich board balanced on the cobbles. Shit. Nothing good can come from the phrase 'Ladies' Night' and especially not 'Laydeez Night'.

You think about turning round and sidling back the way you came, making up an excuse as to why you couldn't attend as you stare through the condensation-streaked windows of the bus. Wonder whether it's appropriate to tell your new coworkers you have accidentally, irrevocably soiled yourself on the way to meet them. No. Too much information. Anything else will do; a leak, a poorly pet, fire, famine or pestilence. Anything other than having to endure this.

Too late. You've been spotted. The sly girl from the desk next to you is waving maniacally from a cluster of particularly vicious looking fowls in the queue. Carefully, you make your way over to them and join their warm huddle. They smell of pheromones, cheap perfume and hairspray so strong it catches in the back of your throat. The inviter laces her arm through yours. It is an iron band that locks you in place. There is no escape.

You try to communicate your distress to the bouncer using only your eyes. But he is checked out. He stares into the middle distance as he takes money with one hand and presses a stamp to the proffered body part with the other. He has the thousand-yard stare of someone traumatised by too many 'laydeez' nights. Rendered an automaton by the trauma of female bonding, he takes your money and never meets your pleading gaze. The Inviter and Sly Girl pull you through the gaping mouth of the entrance. You have forgotten their real names.

The inside of the building is a carbon copy of municipal rooms where you endured certain social interactions you had no choice in attending, forced by a parent who didn't want you to appear rude - a classmate's birthday party, a cousin's engagement announcement, an end of term disco. It shares the same dusty, snide parquet-patterned floors. You half expect a trestle table with a paper tablecloth, laden with a beige buffet of mini sausage rolls, gappy from lack of filling, and time-withered triangle-cut sandwiches. Instead, there is a bar serving plastic glasses of warm, vinegary wine or gin so strong it could strip the enamel from your teeth. You gulp the first one like a shot and resist the urge to retch as it hits the back of your throat and then your empty stomach.

Your colleagues shepherd you to a table in the middle of the room and, before you know it, the house lights have gone down. Only the stage is illuminated. The entire crowd whoops and hollers in anticipation, like a mob of football hooligans. Onto the stage walks a scantily clad man with a straining holdall full of props. The laydeez are almost growling, like they want to tear him apart. Sly Girl snarls and yips like a coyote, waiting for him to take his kit off. To my horror, he obliges.

Over the course of the evening men dressed variously as a firefighter, a ship's captain and a cheap polyester-clad approximation of Tarzan traverse the stage, gyrating and gurning until they are fully nude to the delight of the assembled women. You feel like an anthropologist or a nature documentarian, out of place, on the periphery of all this blood lust.

Halfway through the set, a bevy of servers enters the hall and starts divvying out hot, greasy bags of fish and chips. It seems like a strange choice, but the whole evening has been so odd you're not overly surprised. The woman sitting next to you has ordered a saveloy instead of cod. She wiggles it salaciously to the delight of the rest of the table. You have lost your appetite.

The last act comes on stage. He brings out the customary bag of props, but this time it bears a logo you recognise, that of a sports shop well known for its oversized mugs. Maybe his act is to dribble lukewarm tea down his naked torso. The thought makes you queasier. You don't want to see the oil slick of slightly curdled tea on an already greased, fake tan smeared naked body under the strong lights. Too late. That is exactly what happens. There are biscuits too. Tea break will forever be ruined for you.

Finally, the night ends. You bid farewell to your colleagues until Monday morning. The smile melts from your face as you walk to the bus stop. You spend the entire journey home trawling the job boards for a new position.

Networking

Don't be rude. Fix your face. Your expression is very loud.

The awkwardness comes off you in waves. Like stink lines in a cartoon. You linger at the edges of conversations, like a Peeping Tom – sweating and worried about being caught, having to engage in discourse you neither understand nor care about. You rock from one anxious foot to another. Your smile is sickly, bordering on terminal. Affirmations of comfort muttered under your breath elicit a tight smile of pity from a passer-by. You move away but are unable to outrun your weirdness. Everything in you wants to leave, strains towards the exit like desperately trying to catch the melody of a familiar song through the window of a passing, speeding car.

You notice the fire alarm. Your fingers twitch. *Do it.* The voice behind your eyes is as rough as sandpaper. *Lean in. Let go. DO IT!*

The wave of networkers floods out into the darkening street, the blare of the alarm snapping at their heels like a guard dog triggered into action. In the confusion you slip away from the throng, melt into the darkness of a familiar cut-through. You keep to the edges of the pavement, a cat burglar stealing away from the scene of a crime, trying not to give yourself away with the wheezing of your breath on the steep hill. Finally. Alone.

Peanuts

I.....HATE.... MY....JOB.

Each word expelled every time my foot lands on a differently coloured carpet tile. It is a habitual mantra that I mutter to myself while heading to the communal kitchen. My foot lands in the centre of the tile every time. Step on a crack, break your mother's back. There is no need for me to be heading to the kitchen. The college does not provide free tea or coffee and I have nothing to put in the fridge. I can't afford to go to the cafeteria for lunch either and I know the hot greasy smells emanating from the flung-open doors at lunchtime will be hard to bear. Instead, I have a can of mixed fruit salad for lunch. It was the only can left in the cupboard. Nothing says 'competent adult' like tinned fruit salad for lunch.

Returning to my office with a hot cup of water to explain my absence, I can hear Lois crying as I get to the door. She often cries at the photocopier. Fair. There is always one office contraption which designates itself as your mortal enemy; hers is the photocopier. Lois never wanted my position to become available, a fact I am reminded of every single day and in every single interaction with her. She hates me. It's a fun atmosphere. Her hatred of me has also coloured our boss's opinion of me. I often walk in to their whispered little meetings, a cabal of two, about my supposed lack of performance. While it is true that I am bad at this job, it is less incompetence and more complete lack of training that renders me clueless as to what the job actually entails. Lois should be training me, but she patently refuses to do so. Which is fun.

Our boss calls me into her office. She would like me to show her how to save a file with a different name. I might be bad at my job, but I am not a manager who doesn't know how to use the Save As function. She often asks me why the internet is down. The first time I told her I would ring IT for her. And the second. And the third. If she asks again, I'm going to tell her it's an act of God. Or aliens. Depending how I feel. Sometimes she sits so still at her desk that the motion-activated lights go off, leaving only her face illuminated white by her computer screen. Like Kabuki theatre.

I sit down at my computer and

read the emails that have come in while I have been hopscotching down the corridor and boiling the kettle three times to kill time. I red flag them all, but don't open them. Red flagging at least makes me feel like I am doing something, even if it is just another in a long line of procrastination tools. In an hour, I'll hide in the toilets for a while and try to beat my high score in *Candy Crush Saga* before returning and cracking open my tin of unnaturally coloured fruit in syrup for lunch. Lois sits at the desk next to me. I can feel her stare. It is like being ogled by a bush baby. Turning to her, I watch as her hand dips rhythmically into a bag of honey roasted peanuts. It is 10 a.m. Stare. Crunch. Stare. Crunch. Every crunch seems to tighten the skin of my face. It is like a sunburn of rage.

Slowly, I lower my face to my keyboard like I am gradually deflating.

There is a puncture in my productivity. I rest my forehead on the QWERTY row until the G key is part way up my nose. Leisurely, I rub my face back and forth across the letters and try to imagine that the gentle scratching sound is rain over pebbles or skin against velvet, anything other than the sound of my sanity gently slipping away. The backspace has hit the beginning of the page. The computer boinks at me repeatedly, full of indignation that I would keep on depressing and depressing it. I know the feeling buddy. A burble of laughter slips out between the keys.

'Jhfbuirubjdc ndfifnk' dances across the screen as I continue to drag my face across the keyboard. I'm like a cat rubbing my scent on a trouser leg. On the screen, a purr is forming. I can hear Lois digging her honey roast fingers into the packet over and over. I can feel her eyes. I must be a spectacle as enjoyable as one would find at the circus. Maybe she'll throw peanuts at me, like a child to a pachyderm balancing on a ball in the big top. Maybe it'll be more akin to a stripper with dollar bills. Maybe I'll catch them in my mouth, maybe I'll just let it rain.

The keyboard smells of bread and something slightly salty, the delicate scent of a thousand working lunches crumbling between the keys. I can feel each letter digging into my face, settling in the soft bags under my eyes, pulling my lips up in a sneer, spilling gibberish into my document.

I can hear my boss leaving her office, hear her quick steps up to the edge of my desk. I don't want to stop yet. It is oddly comforting. For the first time since I started this job, I don't want to cry or rage or spit or hide.

"What on earth are you doing?"

she squawks.

I stop. Waiting a moment, I hope the pieces of my mind will shuffle back into some semblance of completeness. They don't. A jigsaw puzzle that has been knocked on the floor by a frustrated child.

"Oh? This? It's ah...a way to get Microsoft exchange back up when your emails go down," I lie.

I can see her thinking about it. She can't glean anything from my expression, it's full of plastic lettering.

"Ah. Oh. OK. Right then," she states and wobbles back to her own office. I watch as she sits down and lowers her permed head to the moulded plastic surface, rubbing her own face along her keyboard.

I smile with a mouth full of keys.

The Office of Petty Revenge

The light coming through the window illuminated the bookcase. It took up the entirety of one wall of the office in which I sat. Stacked along its shelves were hundreds of white binders. The sun glinted off their spines, creating a glare so bright I couldn't read the cramped, tiny handwriting along them. I wondered how much incriminating evidence they held, how many years of prison sentences sat between their solid plastic covers. Vivian watched me as I scoured the bookcase, a wry smile on her face.

"You'd never work out my code," she

said quietly, making me jump. I hadn't noticed her coming in. "That's why people come to me - discretion. Wouldn't be very discrete if I had all their names and numbers written down in a ledger would it?"

"Then what's in the folders?" I asked, tipping my head towards the bookcase.

"Contingency," she said, taking a seat behind the large desk in front of me. "What we do here is not entirely legal, as you can imagine, but this way, as an intermediary, no-one knows what anyone has or hasn't done, has or hasn't asked for. Except me. So, if anyone tries to drop me in the shit, I have the receipts."

She smoothed her hands across the desk and looked at me enquiringly. It was a nice desk. The whole office was nice. It was much nicer than I'd expected for somewhere I'd found on the dark web. It wasn't down some seedy back street, I could see shoppers moving past the frosted windows in the foyer. There was a foyer for God's sake.

I had contacted Vivian because I hated my neighbour and I wanted some form of revenge, nothing too extreme, I didn't want him kneecapped or anything, just …inconvenienced. I had nurtured a litany of petty grievances - waking me up at the crack of dawn on a Sunday to wash his car, parties that were too long and too loud - but the thing that annoyed me the most was parking. I know, how trivial, how small, how quintessentially British. I tried to let it go, I tried to tell myself how insignificant it was but every time he parked his enormous tractor of a 4x4, which was far too large for a small town anyway, across my drive I bridled. I had a tiny car, the kind of car often called a runaround. It was economical with petrol and fitted comfortably into parking spaces. A *sensible* car. It was small but it was not small enough to reverse onto the road past that monster and speed off to undergo whatever errands were required. I often had to perform some fancy manoeuvring and three point turns and other suburban party tricks in order to get off the drive and go. It pissed me off every time.

I didn't want to go over there and have

a conversation. We'd never been close since we'd moved in, never waved hello or passed pleasantries in the street. They'd scowl at or blank me or wait till I'd gone in the house before leaving home. It was a masterclass in passive aggression. And what would I say? There was no law against it. He was parking in front of his own house. He was just doing it in the most inconvenient, inconsiderate way possible. Would I knock on his front door and ask him to stop being a bit of a dick? I was too much of a coward for that. Instead, I fantasised. I thought about sneaking out in the middle of the night and covering the road around his tyres in tacks. I thought about dragging my door key along the shiny sides of the offending vehicle. While reversing I considered "accidentally" losing control and hitting it, letting the force of my motion crumple and crease the bright red wing. I imagined the crunch. It made me smile.

The thing is, he didn't need to park right outside his house, he barely drove the bloody thing. I wondered if it was because the vehicle's sheer size made driving it awkward. On the rare occasions it was not in its spot I would whizz off the drive and proclaim how much smoother it was! How much better! How much easier it made my life! And inwardly cringe at how silly it sounded, even as I felt vindicated at the source of my opprobrium being absent. I made a throw-away account on Reddit and asked users for their opinions on the vengeance I could take. It was full of silly suggestions, some verging and some jumping into full-on illegal activity. I'd log in when having a bad day at work and, stupidly, it made me feel better. I had no intention of acting on any of them, until I saw the most recent post. It was an anonymous account, a jumble of numbers and letters with a blank profile picture. *Why not check out The Office of Petty Revenge?* I couldn't find anything on Google so I messaged the blank account and asked for more details. A foray into the land of the dark web and a few exchanges with Vivian later and I was sitting in her office, The

Office of Petty Revenge.

She explained in vague, and well-rehearsed terms, what the Office did. They would match anyone's request with a facilitator, Vivian working as the intermediary so neither party had details of the other. That would stop any issues relating to blackmail or the requester being contacted by the police should the facilitator be caught. The two parties would remain anonymous to each other but not to Vivian. We talked. We talked and talked and talked for several hours. She knew someone with a junk yard who could deliver me a selection of the most beaten-up, broken-down scrap metal on wheels that the DVLA didn't even know existed so there would be no-one to blame for their appearance in our sleepy suburban road. One could be dumped in his space as soon as he left or a whole stack of them could be deposited in his front garden so he would wake to their teetering tower of metal in the morning. I hadn't laughed as hard as I did with this eloquent, erudite and amoral businesswoman. It took a while, and more money than I expected, but eventually we came up with the perfect idea.

Now I am a code word in one of her white folders in the sun-drenched bookcase, but as I stand in my window with a hot cup of tea warming my hands, watching the road and waiting, I know it was entirely worth it.

About The Author

Melanie Atkinson is a UK horror author living on the south coast with her husband and dog. She can often be found penning horrible little stories in her vegetable garden with a large cup of tea.

For more information see:
https://linktr.ee/melanieatkinsonauthor

Other Titles:

The Last Night In Amsterdam
The Woods Are Full of Eels
Our Lives Are Full of Spectres

Printed in Dunstable, United Kingdom